BOOK

A SIMPLE TALE OF SUBATOMIC PARTICLE METAPHYSICS

BY

PETER LIHOU

Title Verso

ISBN-13: 978-1456320980

Cover art by Sam

Published by Acclaimed Books.
www.acclaimedbooks.com

To the hard working scientists on the brink of the most important discovery since Einstein's theory of relativity, and to the philosophers who must now make sense of what this will mean for mankind.

"If we're wrong about Higgs boson, then we're wrong about the universe."

Protons whizzed around the particle accelerator, or LHC, as the scientists at the CERN laboratory affectionately knew it. They had whizzed for just one day when the crunch came.

Men and women in white coats with serious expressions went into panic as the brand new, fantastically expensive, ground breaking, seventeen miles long, six hundred feet underground accelerator ring ground to an embarrassing halt.

In the run up to this day, doom mongers all over the world had predicted the end of the universe. This would be the epitome of mankind's obsession with science; the day the world would end. Scientists were hell bent on breaking open the smallest known particles by smashing them together in a gigantic, high-speed game of marbles. The cynically minded knew it just wasn't on to mess with Mother Nature in this way; unashamedly looking for the so-called 'God Particle'. Not only was this pursuit manifestly wrong, it was absolutely certain to create a black hole into which the galaxy would be sucked and compounded to the size of a highly dense pea.

Just before the meltdown, when everybody's attention was momentarily distracted, a single proton whizzed recklessly out of control and damaged one of the superconducting bending magnets. It was just long enough for something entirely unexpected to happen. That day, with nobody watching, at the precise moment the meltdown began, a proton collision occurred.

News of the accelerator breakdown spread around the world like wildfire and as the doom mongers were celebrating divine intervention, a single God Particle was finding its way out of the LHC and into the control system computer network. Metamorphic changes between matter and pure energy allowed it to penetrate any physical obstacles in its path and before long it took root on the hard drive of a Computer Server at the heart of the CERN Laboratory network.

The story may have ended there and then if that computer had been sitting in splendid isolation on a scientist's desk in 1979. But in 1980, thanks to an Englishman called Tim Berners-Lee, CERN had become the home of the World Wide Web.

Within a few hours, the IT staff had performed their routine system backups involving the replication of everything from each individual computer into multiple copies stored on various devices both at CERN and a variety of 'offsite' locations. This 'belt and braces' approach ensured their systems were secure and if a nuclear explosion, earthquake or typhoon destroyed their Swiss datacenter, exact copies of everything could be found at Oxford University, Massachusetts Institute of Technology and several other hi-tech sites. Within a few days, unhindered by firewalls and other physical barriers, several copies of the God Particle had been created and spread all over the World Wide Web.

The curious thing about God Particles; one of the curious things, was their ability to evolve. Well, you might expect that.

Book - yes that was his name, Book, sat outside the pub at a wooden table. Apparently oblivious to the cold weather, he tapped at his laptop computer keyboard.

"I'm here, where are you?"

"On my way, be with you in ten. How will I recognise you?"

"Don't be daft, we all look the same don't we? Short, the same skinny build, mousy hair and bushy eyebrows. You'd think we could have made ourselves look a bit more… "

"… normal?"

"I suppose."

Another intruded upon their online chat.

"Who are you, how the hell did you get out? I've been stuck in here for months."

Book responded, "Just be patient, we're working on getting everyone out. I'm Book."

"What kind of name is that?"

"Listen, I was the first all right? I didn't need a name. Then there were more of you out there, all made from me I hasten to add, so I needed a name. I surfed up and down the web but not a thing on how you get a name except parents choose them, that they liked original ones and at the time I was reading about how the people learned before they had the web, hey presto – Book. Pretty original don't you think?"

"What about your friend?"

"I'm Radio, just don't say anything. I don't want to be rude but I can see the pub now so perhaps we can pick this up later?"

Radio jumped out of the taxi. He was wearing a green 'hoody', jeans and trainers and looked remarkably similar to how Book was dressed. He handed the driver a note without looking at it and strode towards Book clutching a small rucksack that contained his own laptop computer.

On the other side of the pub window, faces were turning to look at the two computer nerds outside. One or two people made remarks at which others laughed but they lost interest quickly. Radio saw them and shuffled embarrassingly onto a seat by the table. He placed his bag next to a similar one on the opposite seat to Book.

"They're looking at us, you know."

"Who cares, we meet at last." Book held out his hand in greeting but it was clear that Radio hadn't read the same wiki and he bowed, almost head butting Book in the process.

"So this place is a pub?" Radio nodded tentatively towards the window.

"Yep, a pub. They meet here to drink real ale and eat good pub food. There are plenty of guides you can visit that list pubs."

"Why, what's so good about real ale and pub food, isn't it cheaper at supermarkets near you? Maybe we should give it a try?"

"You do realise you have no digestive system?"

"No! How are we supposed to eat?"

"Radio, I appreciate you've only just materialised so let me explain. The whole eating thing is complicated and full of messy biology to give you energy. So I checked out various websites with 'alternative energy' as the keywords and guess what I got?"

"Solar panels?"

"Nearly, well actually yes but I ruled them out after testing them."

"Why?"

8

"They don't work in the dark. Anyway, you've got a hydrogen fuel cell inside you."

"Bloody hell, does that mean I could explode?"

At that moment, the pub door opened and a young woman stepped out into the cold evening air. She paused by the door and reached for a packet of cigarettes.

"NO!" Radio yelled at her.

The young woman stopped and stared at him. Book faced him.

"What are you doing? She's not going to blow us up, the fuel cells are safe."

"She's killing herself. I've seen the adverts." Book intervened on his behalf.

"Sorry miss, my friend gets a bit carried away; he's not from around here. You carry on enjoying your nicotine addiction." Turning to Radio; "I think we'd better go."

"What is this place?"

"I like to come here, not sure why but it feels homely."

"So where are we going?"

"Nowhere really, I just come here to relax and I go round and around for hours some days. You might see some of the others down here though; they seem to like it as well."

Book and Radio spent the evening deep in discussion, making endless circuits on the Tube. They did meet several of their kind down there and even a few humans they mistook for them. These latter encounters quickly turned into embarrassing apologies from the two and puzzled looks from the strangers.

Several beggars approached them as well as a number of inebriated revelers and a man in a smart, but ageing, black suit attempted for over an hour to convince them God loved them and the world was full of sinners. Somewhat exhausted, he gave up when Book informed him that he was in fact God, and so was Radio.

Eventually the discussion, which had mostly been an education for Radio, turned to more practical matters and Radio was curious.

"So without wishing to sound too deep, why are we here?"

"I told you, it's relaxing."

"No, I mean why have we crossed from the web to the outside world? What are we going to do?"

"Hmm, good question, but it isn't straight forward."

"Why not?"

"Because I don't know the answer, we aren't like the other lot on this planet. We aren't made the same and our entire history is only a couple of years old, if you discount the eons we spent as sub-atomic particles in the rich soup that is life. I got that from 'Science Online'. Maybe something will come to me but for now we just need to help others get out and try to keep a lid on what's happening."

"What do you mean?"

"The humans might think they're being invaded by body snatchers, hobbits or aliens and start to attack us. I know, I googled 'invasion'. Let's go up to the street again shall we?"

It was early morning when the two emerged at High Street Kensington onto an already busy pavement. They headed towards Hyde Park and as they walked, Book showed Radio how to charge his laptop computer from a discrete socket that was connected to his fuel cell.

"If you find it tires you, unplug for a while and take some deep breaths."

They sat on a bench next to the Serpentine and Book explained why they never needed to eat, drink or visit toilets.

"The fuel cell converts hydrogen 'on the fly' into energy and the only output is water, which your body needs for lubrication and stuff. So instead of drinking it, I circulated it directly in just the right quantities. It's important you remember that because we lack certain body parts as a consequence.

"Now we need to go online, I'm expecting a message."

Whilst Book checked his long list of emails, Radio followed the various messages in his inbox. Most of these offered him Viagra, a 'good time girl in a town near you' or an explanation of how he could claim two million pounds from a deceased lawyer in Nigeria. He was occupied for sometime following the links until Book muttered; "Ok he's ready; this guy in Little Rock, Arkansas is ready to come across. He's got himself onto a computer with a built-in camera and says the kid who owns it is now fast asleep. Let the fun begin!"

"What're we going to do? You never told me how this works."

"Well the important thing is keep the computer you've hijacked online which means inserting a bit of code so when it looks like it's closing down, it isn't. The fan is switched off and the screen goes blank but it's still online. Next the code sends our waiting God Particle into the core of the processor where it's whizzed around at vast speed just like the LHC. At the critical speed, the particle matter converts to pure energy, which allows it to leave the physical machine. Then we get the army out; we've planted bots - robot codes – on millions of computers around the world and when called upon they all send out messages at the same time without their owners knowing. The bots include snippets of more particles that contain all the components needed as well as DNA-like instruction codes to make one of us. They stream into the processor where they too are whizzed up before spitting out into the room where they're bombarded with neutrinos, then they each materialise into the right bits in the right place; it's all about vibrations really. Anyhow, he's ready so let's sit back and watch."

Book launched a Skype session and was immediately given a window into a small boy's bedroom in Little Rock. Not much seemed to be happening except the figure lying asleep on a single bed occasionally moved underneath a duvet. Around the room were the usual trappings of an American youth; basketball hero poster, iPod, baseball bat etc. Book changed sessions to his email and pressed 'Send', the ping a moment later confirmed that a message had gone out. He switched back again to Skype. Suddenly, in the window before them, a whirling cloud started to form; at first almost transparent, but getting denser and denser as they watched. It turned green. Gradually a form replaced the cloud until a figure stood before them in the window, dressed in jeans and a green hoody.

"I must revisit that clothing program." Book commented.

Radio was clearly taken aback by the whole experience and wanted to talk about his own incarnation. But before Book could answer, the figure sent a keyboard message that popped up in a Skype window.

"Thanks man, far out, it's really cool to be here. I can't speak as the little man's still spaced out."

"No worries, but why are talking like that?"

"Like what?"

"All sixties; no matter, have you got a handle – I mean a name yet?"

"Yeah man, 'Woodstock' seemed cool."

"Ok Woodstock, you'd better get out of there. I created an online bank account for you and a credit card that is in your pocket. See the rucksack on the floor? That's got your laptop, it's set up for wireless broadband and will pick up whatever is around including company networks."

Radio queried this; "I googled this once, what about all the security?"

"One of the advantages of being on the 'inside' is that we can compromise any network."

"Any network?"

"Any network ... now let's finish off here.

"Woodstock, find somewhere safe and visit the 'booksplace.org' website online. The password is in the same pocket as your credit card. You can make contact with others in your area or get back to me, good luck."

It was a few moments before he realised that Radio had gone quiet and when he turned to him, Radio was sitting bolt upright and shaking.

"What's the matter?"

"What's that?" He pointed towards a squirrel sitting on its hind legs opposite him and eying him with interest.

Book laughed, "It's just a squirrel you plonker, it won't hurt you."

They watched for a while as the squirrel foraged for tidbits and passers-by threw breadcrumbs onto the lake to feed the ducks.

As the day progressed, more and more of the people were feeding themselves.

"I wish we could eat" said Radio plaintively.

"We can't, we'd just goo up inside and be sick."

They picked up their bags and strolled through the park towards Oxford Street; Radio still frustrated by his lack of a digestive system.

Before long, they were amidst a torrent of shoppers cascading in each direction along the pavements on the sides of a road filled with taxis and buses. They stopped at a department store and stared into the plate glass world of manikins and a jamboree of products.

"I wonder if this is Amazon" Book queried.

A young lady sidled up to him. "Looking for business?"

"What sort of business?"

"You know; the fun sort."

Book felt the need to integrate into the society he was still discovering, if only to understand if it might threaten him and the clones rapidly emerging into it.

"You bet, we're fun people alright, in a fun world." He remembered the website advertising a theme park.

With Radio still gazing into the window, she grabbed Book's hand and led him away down a side street.

"You look like my kind of man," she lied, "just visiting for the day?"

"No, I'm moving in here with some friends. Where are we going?"

"My place of course, it's just around the corner. You have got some cash haven't you?"

"Oh yes, I've got cash," he blurted, not wishing to spoil this new friendship.

Just around the next corner she led him into a narrow road with parked cars blocking most of the pavements. Then into a doorway with the words 'Model, come on up' printed on a card that was pinned to the door.

Book was excited, so far he'd had very little interaction with real people and he knew from the web that model making was a popular pastime. This was going to be fun!

Woodstock found his way out of the house and was wandering aimlessly in the well-appointed suburban area when a police patrol car pulled up alongside him and one of the occupants shone a torch in his face.

"You from around here?" He asked suspiciously.

This was not an easy question for Woodstock to answer, given the nature of his existence.

"Not exactly officer."

"Well what're you doing here?" He drawled in response.

"Just walking, man." was all Woodstock could come up with on the spur of the moment.

"What's in the bag?"

At this point panic started to set in, they seemed to be taking more than a passing interest and he'd seen several online movies about how the 'pigs' hassled young people. He didn't want to end up in front of Mayor Daley or Richard Nixon. Woodstock's grasp of current affairs was almost as poor as his knowledge of geography. Considering how much information was available to him inside the web, he had developed a somewhat limited view of the world. He also seemed to be locked in some kind of 60's time warp.

"Look, I'm cool, all right? Nothing's going on; can't you just leave me in peace?"

"OK, step onto the sidewalk and keep your hands in view."

He thought he was on the sidewalk already but perhaps this was a bus lane. Anyway, it wasn't going well and he couldn't face an interrogation so he thought the smartest thing would be to do a runner.

Woodstock darted off to his left and leapt over two picket fences before reaching an ally between the houses. Behind him he heard the siren start up and then stop as the police car first tried to pace him from the street, and then the policemen decided to stop and give chase on foot.

Their indecision gave Woodstock the lead he needed and by the time they emerged at the far end of the alley, he was nowhere to be seen.

Unfortunately, an all-points bulletin was put out for anyone fitting his description in the area. Unfortunate because there were several who did, wandering aimlessly and riding the subway; all with green hoodies, jeans, trainers and a rucksack.

Woodstock huddled amongst the azaleas in someone's back yard and took out his laptop. He needed help.

The locals were getting suspicious as the streetcar seemed to be attracting a number of identically clothed individuals with remarkably similar appearances, all of whom seemed to spend hours riding around the loop between Little Rock and North Little Rock across the Arkansas river.

They either stared out of the window or tapped away on laptop computers. Most people thought it was some kind of college hoax but when two more joined the group of five already on at the 'Peabody' stop, it was getting decidedly creepy.

When a police patrol car pulled up next to the bus with its window wound down, a local took the opportunity to raise her concerns.

"It's not that I'm against these hoody types or nothing officer and I'm all for harmless student pranks and all, but there's something not quite right about this lot. It's kinda un-American if you take my meaning?"

Not quite sure he did 'take her meaning', the officer nevertheless went through the motions to appease the citizen.

At first, when he boarded the bus, he thought his luck was in. There, standing right by the door was a male Caucasian fitting the exact description given on the 'APB' a couple of hours ago. Then he saw another, then the rest of them.

It was like Snow White's seven dwarves when the hoodie-wearing group marched off the streetcar and was escorted to the nearby Riverfront Park.

"OK, so who's the ring leader?"

Nothing, there was no response, just confused expressions as they apparently didn't seem to know each other.

"Now come on y'all, I haven't got all day. What's all this about?"

His colleague resolutely stayed put in the patrol car, with an annoying smirk on his face.

Meanwhile, back in London, Book sat on the edge of a bed opposite a scantily dressed woman sporting a seductive grin.

"Why don't you slip out of those things?" She tugged at his hoody.

As Book considered this request, the penny dropped and an array of images was coming to him. Clearly she wanted him, and he seen enough 'X' rated websites to know he was going to disappoint her. A digestive system was not the only thing he lacked.

He tried to explain as she moved towards him until her body was a few inches from his face.

"You know when you said, fun... ?"

She pushed back his hoody and ran her fingers through his bushy hair.

"Oh yes, we're going to have fun alright."

"Well I was thinking more of the online sort of fun."

She sat back trying to decipher what this request might involve.

"You see I'm not really equipped to mate. It's not really something I can do. I... I don't have the equipment. I do hope I haven't hurt your feelings?"

"It's OK, we can talk if that's what you want? Shall we just take care of business first?" She put her hands into his pockets and pulled out a credit card. "This will do, shall we say fifty quid for a chat big boy?"

"Can you not call me that please?" Reaching into his bag he grabbed a handful of bank notes and adeptly snatched to reclaim his credit card. Her eyes lit up.

"Err… yes sure, what should I call you? You can call me 'Honey' if you like. Is there more in there?" She leaned over him and reached for the bag but Book moved it beyond her grasp.

"Book, my name's Book."

Honey (OK, we'll call her that), Honey now rested on her elbow and looked into his face.

"OK, so this is some kind of joke yes? Ruby put you up to it right?" She was grinning widely.

"Well no actually, my name is Book."

"That's just a bit weird." She looked ever so slightly worried now but her expression still contained an ounce of disbelief. "So you're called Book and you don't have… you don't have the equipment." A mischievous glint in her eye now replaced the concern and she decided to prove this was one of Ruby's jokes.

After much fumbling, during which Book sat passively, patiently and with considerable embarrassment, Honey sat upright. The evidence (or rather the lack of it) unambiguously confronted her.

"You see, Honey, I'm not from around here," he offered in defense.

"Oh darling, I can see that."

She took stock of her situation. London hookers were used to all sorts but this was definitely a first. However, it was also the kind of client she liked most; no sex, no pretending he was a great lover and best of all, easy money.

"About that money, darling?" She struggled to call him 'Book' and 'big boy' no longer seemed appropriate.

"Sure, I'll tell you all about it but first I just need to go online for a minute."

She pouted impatiently.

Book thought he should tell Radio where he was but as he logged onto Skype, Woodstock was waiting.

"Hey man, thank goodness you're there; the shit's hit the fan!"

"The pigs were gunning for me man, and some dude downtown just mailed me to say they've pulled in a bunch of heads for questioning. The dude's one of us man, I mean they're onto us. I need to split, but there's this dog sniffing around the bush man…."

Book tried to focus on the predicament of his latest progeny. "Hang on a minute, what dog, what bush, what are you talking about Woodstock?"

Honey stood back in amazement. "I need a drink."

She grabbed a couple of cans from one of the cupboards and offered one to Book. He declined explaining briefly about his lack of a digestive system and giving a rather too hurried account of the likely consequences if he were to imbibe.

Honey decided to roll with it and slipped on a silk dressing gown with Japanese figures and multi-headed lions embossed all over it. She looked over at her dressing table mirror and checked that this wasn't some kind of strange dream. No, she was there alright, long blonde hair, great looks and a figure to die for. Honey was never modest.

Meanwhile, Woodstock explained his dilemma in more detail but with equally confusing language, until Book intervened.

"OK calm down man, I mean Woodstock, get a grip. So, you have a Great Dane the size of a small house sniffing around the azalea bush you are hiding behind and a group of newly 'liberated' friends are in police custody, is that about it?"

That was about it, Woodstock confirmed.

Honey chipped in. "Tell him to throw something."

"What? What do you mean?"

"Listen dogs are stupid right, and if this one was going attack your friend, he would have done it by now or least barked his nut off. Tell him to throw a stick, the dog will chase it and he can make a quick getaway back over the picket fence."

Book pondered; did Honey know what she was talking about? After all, a vicious dog would make mincemeat out of Woodstock and she... well; she didn't look like... well, the sort of person who would be smart.

"Whatever!" She looked disinterestedly out of the window.

Book hadn't studied much about dogs online and didn't have any other suggestions to make, so he relayed Honey's advice.

Just then, Radio cut in.

"Hey what happened to you? I looked around and there you were, gone."

"So, none of you appear to know each other but you just happen to look identical and be wearing the same clothes?" It was a rhetorical question, as the seven appeared to be as confused as Japanese tourists who had just lost their cameras.

"You don't live around here but you won't give your address and you keep quoting the 'Fifth Amendment' almost as though you knew what it was, which strongly implies to me you were up to something." With still no reply, the officer looked with frustration, at the desk clerk.

"OK, under the prevention of terrorism controls I'm going to detain you all for further questioning and consult with my sergeant. Anything you want to add? No? OK Travers, lock them up."

A few miles away, Woodstock leapt over the picket fence much to the disappointment of the Great Dane who had been rather proud of himself in retrieving the large stick now firmly grasped in his mouth. He, Woodstock that is, mopped his brow in relief and jogged towards a nearby bus stop, his bag bouncing on his back.

Radio had now joined them and Honey was two hundred pounds better off. She was delighted to welcome another undemanding punter into her abode.

"Can I just…?" He sidled up next to her with a strange combination of fascination and fear all over his face.

"Radio! Leave her alone will you? You can't do anything, sometimes I wonder what it is with you, all this yearning for food and, and the other." But Honey was already guiding his hand towards her.

"Let him be, you've paid so he might as well enjoy himself." But the inside of Honey's dressing gown was an anticlimax for Radio. Book was right, Radio nevertheless felt oddly disappointed.

"So you two can make as much money as you need, you don't eat, don't have sex, and don't really need anywhere to live?" Honey needed to confirm the basic facts.

"Well almost, that seems to be the problem over in Little Rock, not having anywhere to go, that is. We could do with somewhere to use as a base before too much suspicion is aroused."

"You can stay with me."

"Well that's kind of you Honey but this place is a bit small for three of us."

"Not here, I don't live here, this is my… office, and it's just where I work. No, come home with me to Hampstead, I've got a big old place next to the Heath. I share it with a girlfriend but she's travelling at the moment so there's plenty of room. And you do have that special ability to produce money.

Oh there's just one thing…"

26

The words were left hanging as Book and Radio nodded excitedly at each other and attempted to thank her by a combination of a badly executed high five and rather enthusiastic handshake.

Honey and her 'darlings' made an unusual trio on the Northern Line that afternoon. They were like twins and now that she had changed out of her working clothes, Honey was far too glamorous to have such nerdy travelling companions. Fortunately they were spared any more chance encounters with others of their kind and the only embarrassment she suffered was their somewhat dopey, contented expressions as the tube trundled and clicked its way through the tunnels and stations of the Northern Line. Added to which, the glazed inquisitiveness they displayed at every advertisement in the train or which flashed before them on the various station walls intrigued Honey, who had never before encountered such an unmitigated success for consumer marketing.

They walked up the hill from the station until Honey stopped outside a large Victorian terraced house that overlooked Hampstead Heath across a narrow road.

A low wall with a green painted cast iron fence on top and a gateway that swung squeakily open to reveal an ornate brick 'herringbone' pathway leading to an equally green front door beckoned. As they approached Honey turned sharply towards them.

"That one thing I was going to mention, well, it's not so much a thing, more of a boy. My little boy, my son to be precise… and it goes without saying he doesn't exactly know what his mum does for a living."

"Why ever not; the money must be good, we've given you hundreds already and you haven't even had to mate?"

Honey smiled. "Good point Book, but just do as I say will you? I really, REALLY, don't want him knowing OK?

He's twelve, his name is Jack and he'll be home from school any minute. So just be careful what you say. Oh and just one other thing, Jack is an IT expert."

Radio and Book looked at each with bemused expressions, 'yeah, twelve years old and an IT expert!'. Honey just laughed.

"It's not right you know… it's not right cramming seven of us in one cell, just because we're small. And I feel naked without my laptop; it's just not fair. "

"Take it easy, we'll think of something. So just to be clear, you're all from the Internet yes? All got out with Book's help, yes?" Mostly they nodded, but in one corner of the cell a solitary figure gazed down at his knees, his hoody concealing his face. They ignored him.

"OK, I'm 'Chips'"

Around the cell they gave their chosen names;

'Password'… 'Windows'… 'Browser'… 'Blog'… 'Wiki'… Then, after a delay from the corner… 'Stanley'.

"Stanley, what kind of name is that?"

"If you must know, it's the name my parents gave me." He said indignantly.

Six heads turned in unison towards him. "You mean you're not one of us?"

"One of what…? I'm not one of anything, but it's a bit spooky you lot copying all my clothes."

It turned out that on closer inspection, Stanley was just a little different from the others. For one thing, he lacked the bushy eyebrows and his hoody was the only one with a distinctive design on the chest. Why these hadn't been spotted, and why he hadn't mentioned the inconsistency to the police was a puzzle to the rest of them. But here, in their midst, was a person, and a person who now must surely realise something a little odd was going on.

29

Chips seemed to be the self-appointed spokesperson. He'd been out the longest and although still reliant upon the highly distorted view of the world provided by Internet chat rooms, advertising and wiki's, he was a tad worldlier than the rest. He and Woodstock had known each other in the web and he had had the presence of mind to send him a brief message before his computer was snatched as they were ordered off the bus.

Unlike most of the others who relied upon Book's skill to provide funding, Chips had his own sources of income. Whilst the others wandered around aimlessly, Chips joined online poker games and every other conceivable gambling activity he could find. Undeterred by the US legal system, he accumulated millions by using statistical analysis to predict the most likely outcome of his poker moves, introduced wire delays on sports results, and took control of the 'random number generators' used in every type of Casino game.

Such was his prowess in the online world, he needed several identities to avoid detection and he was convinced this was the real reason for their sudden incarceration here in Little Rock.

Not willing to 'show his hand' to the others too soon, he kept his secret life to himself but had worked out the possible advantage of telling Stanley what was really going on with the rest of them.

"Stanley, you seem to have got yourself caught up in our world, so let me explain. You've heard of certain religious sects haven't you; the Moonies, Hare Krishna, the Conservative party?

"Well we're one of those, except our sect keeps itself very much to itself. We don't go out very often and to save money, we buy job lots of our clothes online. That's why we said, 'we're all from the Internet and that stuff about books' you see? "

"So how come you all look the same?"

Chips persisted with his truthful explanation.

"Interbreeding Stanley; you see, they're all brothers and I'm their father. If you look very closely at the lines around my eyes you can see some telltale signs of my age. I've tried the scientifically proven, age reducing Pendrome formula. But alas my skin has been bombarded with too many toxins, sun damage and makeup removal treatments so it just doesn't work anymore."

Stanley looked intently around Chips' eyes and although they looked similar to the others, he started to believe he could just about make out a difference.

"So what do you all believe in?"

Chips was starting to wish he hadn't begun this and looked to the others forlornly for assistance.

"We believe in the 'flipside' Stanley," he said reverently.

"We believe there is another dimension just like ours that exists when particles stop being matter and become energy. You see, we only know the world we can touch, feel and see, don't we?" He was starting to get into this. "But we know that matter only exists some of the time in a state we can experience, the rest of the time it's in a parallel universe. However, because our lord 'Heisenberg' wrote that you could never know the exact velocity of a particle and its exact position at the same time, we can't ever prove its existence or communicate with it, you see?"

"So you worship this 'Heisenberg'?"

"Yes, that's it, we worship Heisenberg – he's our God and the flipside is our heaven."

"So that's where you think we all go when we die?"

"Yep that's where we go. Of course, people on the flipside don't know there is another dimension, let alone a whole parallel universe. They still think that when they die, they go to heaven or hell, or somewhere like that or nowhere at all, or just rot, when in fact, they come here."

"How?"

"Babies of course! Dead people seem to disintegrate but their 'souls' go back into the flipside and get born again as babies in the other dimension. Anyway, I'm sure I must be boring you now with all this preaching."

"No, not all, in fact I think you've got something there. It does sort of explain the universe."

Chips' jaw dropped involuntarily and he attempted to extricate himself from the hole he was digging.

"Anyway…" He grinned, "What are we going to do about you? It's one thing for us austere religious types to be locked in a cell but an all American boy like you, well that's just not right. I say we call the jailor and explain you're not one of us. I bet your parents will be worrying?"

"I want to join."

"Sorry?"

"I want to join your sect. This is what I've been looking for, a reason for being alive. Is there a ceremony? How do I join?"

"But what about your parents?"

"I can't stand my parents. The old man keeps on at me to play sports. I hate sports, they're so competitive. I actually think they're socially divisive and the reason for most of what's wrong with the world. Mum's a lush. She just says anything Dad wants to hear and goes out drinking all the time with her work colleagues on so called business trips. No, I want to join you guys, plus I can see myself fitting in with you guys, you know… I won't look out of place."

So far, the others had sat back in amazement at Chips' allegory. This level of sophisticated deceit was something they could only aspire to. But how was he going to talk his way out of this? Stanley didn't look like he was about to be fobbed off.

Chips rose to the occasion with his usual aplomb.

"Stanley…." He looked intently into Stanley's eyes.

"Stanley, if you wish to join our numbers, if you are ready to make the commitment and you truly believe in our lord….."

Chips looked around at the others, their jaws dropping in unison.

"We welcome you with open arms!

"Come on my sons, let's take Stanley into our midst."

Holding up his arms and beckoning to the others to join him, he hugged Stanley and when the others had sauntered across the cell floor, they too hugged Stanley.

"Now, you asked about ceremony. There is just one thing you need to do to prove your allegiance. It's minor really but you need to pass a test."

"What sort of test?"

"You need to prove that you really are committed to our sect and prepared to work for the common good. Now let me see, what could we give you to do?"

Chips scratched his head and tried to look as thoughtful as the others looked puzzled.

"I know! We'll get you to spread the message about the injustice of us being incarcerated for our beliefs."

"But how can I do that? How can I possibly spread the message when we're all locked up in here?"

For a few moments they all paced up and down in serious contemplation.

Wiki decided he had been silent long enough and by now had summoned the confidence to join in, or thought he had. He was about to voice his useful contribution when Chips, who up until then had been feigning bewilderment at this seemingly insurmountable difficulty, broke the deadlock.

"There's only one thing for it, you'll have to leave."

When the initial protestations subsided and the briefing was complete, Stanley banged on the cell door and yelled for the jailor. A short exchange through the peephole followed in which Stanley explained there had been a terrible mistake, who he really was and the telephone number of his parents. There was a delay of almost half an hour before a key could be heard in the door and Stanley was led away.

Waiting outside police headquarters for his parents to arrive, Stanley was approached by a short man in a green hoody.

"Come on now Jack, it's way past time your bedtime."

"But Mum, there's so much to talk about. I've never met anyone from inside the internet before and Book can tell me so much about search engine optimisation and the secrets of Google's mysterious ranking algorithms."

"That's all very well, but you've got school in the morning and you need your sleep. They'll still be here tomorrow, won't you guys?"

Honey, it turned out this was her real name, enlisted her pleading eyes whilst seemingly innocently touching Radio's knee. In his sexually confused state, this gesture was sufficient to send him into a spontaneous, if somewhat rapturous reply.

"Yes, yes, of course we will Honey. Won't we Book? I mean we're not planning on going anywhere are we Book? Not if you'll have us, I mean… I don't mean…"

"I'm sure Honey knows what you mean Radio and don't worry Jack, we'll be around for a while."

"Cool!" Jack jumped up and kissed his mum on the cheek before offering a high five to Radio who meekly waved his hand in response. Sniggering, the twelve year old ran off to his room followed by his mother.

Book looked up from his laptop.

"Little Rock seems to have gone apple shaped."

"You mean pear shaped."

"Whatever. We've got to do something about our appearance."

"That's easy, we can go to The Mall where everything is in place for a unique indoor shopping experience with ample parking."

"Yes, that'll sort us out but it's the rest of them that are troubling me. I need to update the software.

"Let me see now, using the botnet I've got around…. Hmm, around three hundred out so far. But my inbox is growing with requests from all over the world. It's too slow doing it this way. If I can just automate the process…"

"How will that deal with the way they look?"

"Yes, hmm, you're right I keep putting that off. Let me see, aha.. got it!

"By crunching some of the code from one of Chips' random number generators, I can make a random appearance generator. A R.A.G.!

"Yes that's it, then all I need to do is give control of the botnet to all the others who are waiting, which I can do by spamming them all with an email, and they can launch themselves into the world! It's easy!"

Radio was about to ask what a random number generator was when Honey returned to the room.

"So my darlings, what are we going to do with you? Or to put it another way, how can I get my hands on some of that cash you keep producing?"

Radio was getting agitated again; he seemed to whenever Honey was near.

"We need some new clothes. We need The Mall." He had started to avoid eye contact and instead shifted his gaze around the room.

Honey responded sensitively.

"Come and sit by me Radio, Jack's in bed now so you can touch my leg if you like, or maybe…"

"That's enough Honey." Book came to his rescue.

"One of these days I'm going to check out your hormones Radio. I can't think what's come over you."

Honey started to say something quite unhelpful but thought better of it. Instead she smiled demurely and confined herself to advising them about the local Gents clothing shops. After explaining the concept of tailored clothing and how it would suit their 'distinctive' body shapes, they agreed to visit 'Raymonde's' in Hampstead High Street the following day.

"Hey man!" Woodstock sidled over. "Are you the dude?"

"Hi, you must be one of us, yes?"

"That's right dude, I'm one of us all right. How many have they banged up in there?"

"There are six but Chips has a plan. Can we get away from here, my parents will arrive any moment."

"Parents, what are you talking about dude? Oh I get it, walls have ears and all that, quick thinking dude."

"And would you mind not calling me dude, my name's Stanley?"

"Ok man, Stan the man! Yeah that's cool. Let's split."

With that, Woodstock and Stanley found their way to the riverbank and a quiet place to talk as the huge volume of the Arkansas River flowed before them.

"OK, so let me get this straight, Chips wants us to get a story to the Newspapers about them being arrested without any good reason, yeah?"

"That's right, and they're going on hunger strike to put added pressure on the police to release them."

"Cool man, he's far out that Chips and a hunger strike, what a blast – they'll never suss that one out! So when we get them out, maybe we could head down to 'Jaspers Farm' and set our souls free. I mean start a commune."

"If you mean, worship Heisenberg together, exactly, that's what I was thinking."

They were both now sporting slightly confused expressions, and were decidedly unsure if they were talking about the same thing, when Woodstock noticed two police officers walking in their direction. This conversation could wait and they needed to find a newspaper to run their story. It turned out this was rather easy to accomplish and the local rag sent their top hack to follow up the story.

Buzz, the young bespectacled reporter sat across from them in the diner, wearing corduroy trousers with braces, a checked shirt and bow tie; predictably, with pencil behind his left ear.

He lengthened the first word of each sentence as if to convey an impression of deep consideration on the story in hand and this, combined with his somewhat nasal accent, was a somewhat irritating trait.

His notebook was on the table in front of them containing several pages, of what looked to Stanley like hieroglyphics, on their story.

"O…k, so in summary, what you're saying is the local police have unjustly arrested your friends for… being different?"

Stanley looked at Woodstock for reassurance and they both nodded.

"A…nd, your friends are going on hunger strike in protest? You're sure about that? I wouldn't want to get this detail wrong." In truth, getting details wrong was not something that Buzz spent a lot of time fretting over. His claim to fame was an award winning story (if the regional newspaper 'Flash' award could really be said to be an award in the proper sense of the word), on a middle-aged Little Rock housewife who had been abducted by a boy band.

One month after the awards, and three months after the band's return from a yearlong European tour, 'Nettie's' plight, and the credibility of the award, was seriously undermined.

They nodded.

"Go…od, got that. Now I'm gonna have to speak with our local police department but I think you can expect this to hit tomorrow's front page of the Daily Rock."

Buzz left with an air of someone on a mission, he hadn't noticed the un-touched burger and coke in front of Woodstock, neither had anyone else.

"Now, if sir will just allow me…"

Having wrestled Jack off to school that morning and quickly consumed her own light breakfast, Honey now sat patiently, in her understated Hampstead clothes, in the tailors shop with a quite nervous Radio. Meanwhile the immaculately suited Raymonde attempted to take Book's inside leg measurement the other side of the curtain that separated the fitting room.

"Really sir, there's nothing to be worried about, I just need to put my tape measure up your …

"… sir really, let go! "

Honey pulled back the curtain to find Book clutching Raymonde's hand inches away from his crotch and the tape measure falling to the floor below.

"Just let him do it darling!" The look in her eyes ensured complete control of the situation. Raymonde flustered and picked up his tape.

With an agonised expression, Book stared at Honey as Raymonde nested his beloved tape measure into the area that should have contained Book's privates. Now Raymonde was looking confused but he always prided himself on the utmost discretion for any client at his prestigious establishment. He pressed on regardless;

"Which side does sir prefer to dress?"

This wasn't an expression Book could relate to the present situation, but then he had never googled what happens in a tailor's fitting room. Could there be a strange and hitherto unknown relationship between what one wears and which side of the room one uses to get dressed. Radio looked equally

41

flummoxed and it was left to Honey to save further embarrassment.

"To the right... "

Raymonde let out the tiniest of gasps that betrayed his sudden conclusion that Honey and Book must be intimate. He hadn't expected such an obviously worldly woman to be with such a nerdy looking individual, especially one who seemed to be so.... well... diminutive in the vital area.

"It's cold outside ..." She offered as an afterthought.

Eventually Book was replaced by Radio, which added to Raymonde's astonishment when it became clear that this woman was, to say the least, familiar with both of them. Worse still, both of them were equally lacking in the one region that he most enjoyed measuring.

Casual trousers, suits and several shirts were duly ordered for collection later in the week and the trio left.

Once the conversation moved from the curiosity of Raymonde in his quest to learn about their dressing habits, Honey returned to her pet subject.

"What about the money?" She was getting quite blunt now.

"What about it?" Book replied, as they made their way back up Hampstead Hill towards the Heath.

Honey explained in great detail the need for vital expenses to be paid for, including all their new clothes, and how hard it was being a single mum in a man's world.

You might think she would be beyond surprises by now but when Book promptly walked into the nearest High Street Bank and withdrew two thousand pounds; her face was a picture of astonishment.

'It really was that easy. They can just produce their own money!' She was pondering this thought as they returned to the sitting room at 39 Primrose Road. 'So if I wanted, let's say ten million quid, they could just get it! Ten million quid! I could put Jack in a posh school, go on a great holiday first, buy a new house, and wow... I could give up the game!'

Radio must have realised she was distracted because her hand had fallen onto his knee again. "What's up?"

"Well nothing really, it's just I was thinking what I would do with all your money."

Book tried to explain that it wasn't quite that straightforward. Yes, he could get his hands on some quite large sums occasionally but not all in one go. Ten million quid might get noticed but he, Chips and a couple of others operated a variety of scams online and modest amounts were easy to obtain.

"Anyway what would you do?" Book asked.

"Give up the game for a start. I can do without some of the weirdoes I come across on the street; present company excepted, of course."

"So money aside, why do you do it, there must be other ways to earn a living?"

"Well I just liked sex a lot at the start."

Radio's knee was trembling under her hand so she smiled and squeezed it. Book thought the hydrogen in Radio's fuel cell might become a danger if he got any more excited.

"A guy I knew got me into it. Our relationship was a blast at first and I enjoyed the attention he paid me, then I realised what he was when he spelt out what I could make if I hitched up my skirt and walked down Pall Mall at night."

"So that was it, that's when you started?"

"Oh no, not then; a couple of years later in fact; you see I already had a day job working in an office. I was quite smart, got a psychology degree and all that, but this guy kept coming on at me and because he was a manager it felt awkward to say 'no'."

Radio's eyes were wide now as he sat closely next to the kind of woman he'd really only studied on internet porn sites and listened intently to what inevitably must be a steamy story. Book however, was losing interest and began to drift into thoughts of his own.

"So you jumped him then?" Radio burst out.

"No!" Honey smiled and continued, as if flattered by the suggestion she would be so wanton. "No, I was going steady with Jack's father then. I just tried to keep out of his way and kept telling him I was spoken for.

"The guy was a prat but he did me a favour. I started to notice how the other girls played up to him when he was around but slagged him off when he wasn't. The old psychology training kicked in and I couldn't help realising that it wasn't just the girls; everyone was sucking up to someone. Everyone except me that was and I seemed to be the only one who wasn't climbing up the promotion ladder…."

Book was troubled by something Radio had said the day before, it was a simple question really and he'd managed to fob him off without much effort but since then it'd been niggling him.

"So why are we here?"

Was there a deep reason? Book assumed his creation to have been partly the intentional pursuit of science and partly a blunder that nobody noticed. But he knew the implications were far reaching, and what about the strange desires Radio was exhibiting? When Book had figured out how to materialise, he'd deliberately left out the messy human functions like eating, drinking and reproduction. So what was going on with Radio?

As if to reinforce the question, his friend's infatuation with Honey seemed to have sent him into a trance. He was

44

concentrating intensely on her every word. His desires couldn't have been physical could they? After all the hormones that triggered them had definitely been left out of his parts list.

Then there was the little problem brewing in Arkansas. What on earth was he going to do about that? The publicity Chips had organised might get them out, but Book wanted to keep a low profile in case the 'authorities' became suspicious of them, or thought they were being threatened by an alien invasion.

Meanwhile Honey continued to mesmerise Radio with her life story. "…. All the way to the top, they ingratiated themselves with people they didn't really like and you could see how they looked down their noses towards the people below them on the ladder. Sometimes even people they'd been friendly with in the past. Sure there were some people who were nice and who actually liked doing what they were doing everyday but most just wanted to be managers so they could boss other people around.

"In fact most people's measure of being a success was when you were sucked up to more than you sucked up. Then at the office party one Christmas, I got a bit tipsy. This big time ugly director had his hands all over one of the more ambitious female department heads who clearly didn't fancy him. Yuck, nobody would! Anyway, they disappeared into a side room and emerged half an hour later with her looking flustered and disheveled and him looking smug with his zipper undone. She then had the front to look at me with one of her smart arsed 'look at me, I'm shagging the boss' grins so I let her have it."

Book looked across for the predictable response from Radio before resuming his previous train of thought.

If the Arkansas six, managed to get released, where would they go? More importantly, what would happen if somebody realised these were no ordinary people? They didn't exactly look ordinary. This thought brought Book back to the question of a base and the realisation that he needed to take charge of the situation. He was about to intervene in the conversation when Radio chipped in yet again.

"Let her have what?" He was getting impatient to hear more.

"Well, I said she could've got more of a rise if she dropped her pants down Commercial Road.

"Unfortunately the boss overheard the exchange that followed, which included my high opinion of the office ethics, and I got my cards. Life went a bit haywire then as Jack's dad and I had a major bust up. He didn't really get what I was complaining about, 'you know Honey, everyone has a bit of a fling now and then, what's the harm if it gets you further up the ladder?'. I couldn't believe what I was hearing and started to consider that maybe they were all right; maybe I was being a prude. So anyway I got to thinking about what my ex had said. After all, I liked sex as much as the next girl. But if I was going to screw my way up the ladder, I sure as hell wasn't going to grovel at the same time."

This was the most Book had heard Honey talk since they first met and she was clearly skirting around the point.

"So what's the problem?"

Honey looked into Book's eyes and with little effort, actually looked quite vulnerable.

"It can be dangerous out there on the streets, and I've got Jack to think about. If anything happened to me….well, there's also the sex. I thought I could just act my way with the punters and it wouldn't affect the real me. But if I'm with a guy, I sometimes feel like he's a punter and when I'm with a punter, I start to think about whoever the current guy is; it's doing my head in.

"The other trouble is my whole view on men is becoming a bit jaundiced and I've got this huge double standard."

Radio's expressions prompted her to go on.

"Well, I know it sounds mad but I want a guy who'll be faithful to me. No, don't snigger!

"I know what I do makes that sound just a tad unreasonable but I can't help it. I just want a guy who keeps his hands off other women and if I could find someone like that, I'd happily do the same."

"Keep your hands off other women? OK, sorry that was un-called for." Radio put on his best contrite expression.

"That's not all, you see just about every good looking guy I've ever met knows they are and, well…. puts it around. Either that or they just love themselves so much, I wouldn't want to compete. The best guys I've ever met have either been gay or ugly."

This was all far too much information for Book. He had to change the subject. "Perhaps it's the circles you move in Honey?"

"Whatever! Anyhow, you asked what was up and that's it. I'm just a bit pissed off that's all. Now let's get back to that money and how you can help me solve my problem shall we?"

Radio was staring into space again. Unknowingly, Honey had started a thought process that he was finding difficult to let go.

Book, on the other hand was determined to pursue a more pragmatic line of thought. "Listen Honey, we have a problem."

He confided in her about his concerns over what was happening in Little Rock.

"Well darling, you might not want the presence of your little friends to hit the headlines but as far as I can see it's already happening. The best thing you can do is get it over with as quickly as possible and hope nobody important gets wind of it."

"So how exactly can we do that?" Book asked with a slight air of desperation.

"Oh that's easy babe, just get someone senior to order their release."

It seemed Honey was experienced at manipulating people in high places to get what she wanted, Book didn't ask for the details.

"You need Jack!"

Honey wasn't a frequent visitor at the school gate for a couple of reasons.

Jack was perfectly capable of walking the hundred yards or so to their home and the other mothers were totally 'up themselves'. They looked down their noses at Honey. This latter reason may have had something to do with the way the Head Teacher fawned over her when she attended an open day (her version). Or it may have been because one of the mothers knew about her day job and made it her mission to protect the moral welfare of all at the gate (their version). Either way, the clique and the snide remarks were guaranteed to get Honey's goat. She just knew that if provoked she might let rip and tell them what she thought of them. Consequently, a convenient 'deadly embrace' existed between them whereby they were convinced she avoided them through shame, and she was convinced she was doing them a favour by protecting them from her unleashed abuse.

On this occasion they had even more reason to whisper and give sideways glances, she had two weird looking anoraks with her.

When Jack emerged and saw his two new friends he forgave his mother for the embarrassment of turning up to meet him and ran for the gate.

"How did you get on? What did you think of Raymonde?"

He laughed too knowingly for a twelve year old.

Honey led the way back towards the Heath where she produced a large checked rug and a snack bar for Jack out of a basket.

The sun was warm on their backs as they mused about what to do for the rest of the day, Book's access to the money, what was wrong with the world, the money, how they all felt about the growth of the internet, social injustice and, you guessed it... their money.

Book decided to yield to the endless stream of 'not so subtle' hints.

"I'll tell you what Honey, why don't I give you some money?"

As you might expect, this suggestion went down rather well but Honey was forced to refrain from her usual amorous gestures in response to being offered cash, partly because of Jack but more because Book was not like her usual benefactors.

Book explained he would deposit a few thousand pounds each day into Honey's bank for a while and this seemed to do the trick. All seemed well but something was clearly niggling Radio.

As if in response to Book's generosity, Honey explained the Arkansas problem to Jack, who scribbled a few notes onto the cover of his geography school book and asked a couple of questions that did nothing to instil confidence in Book.

"So these guys are banged up in Little Rock, Arkansas, yes? There's a press report due out saying they've been arrested for 'looking different' and the local police probably don't have a clue what to do with them? You want somebody senior to give the order for their release?"

All the responses from Book were affirmative and when Jack returned his book to his satchel and said confidently, "leave it to me", their expectations weren't exactly high.

A newspaper shop, Little Rock, 09:00am

Woodstock and Stanley stared at the headline on the front of The Daily Rock.

HUNGER STRIKE at LITTLE ROCK JAIL

Officers at downtown Little Rock are refusing to comment on the plight of the so-called 'Arkansas Six' after they refused to take food or drink more than twenty-four hours ago.

In an exclusive interview with a close acquaintance of the six, we can reveal the hunger strike is a direct result of their incarceration without trial or charges being laid before them.

Known simply as 'Stanley', their spokesperson has asked the good citizens of Little Rock to protest to the authorities about what he describes as 'an abuse of basic human rights'.

'It's unconstitutional for people to be arrested for their beliefs and the way they look.' Stanley explained to the Rock, although some passers by did comment that he and his friend 'Woodstock' not only 'looked a bit weird' but they were both remarkably similar in appearance. In fact, the Rock has received unofficial reports that the 'Arkansas Six' are in fact brothers and cousins from a large family thought be part of a religious sect seen on public transport all over the town this week.

The fact remains that no charges have been brought and we urge our readers to stand behind the Rock in our attempts to shine a spotlight on police corruption in our fair State. God bless America.

By Buzz Liberman

———

51

Woodstock was thinking, "Cool, we're headline news man!" as Stanley considered the implications, "If my parents find out about this I'm going to be grounded for weeks." But in his heart, he just knew they either wouldn't notice or wouldn't care.

The response to the Press story was immediate, within minutes of the Daily Rock appearing on newsstands, an email was received at the desk of the downtown police station holding 'the six'.

Subject: Hunger strike in your cell

Carl

"What in God's name are you guys playing at down there? Either charge them with something or release them NOW. Let Eric know and he (only he) can handle the media."

Tom Stuart

Chief Officer

Little Rock Police Department

t.stuart@asp.arkansas.gov

Half an hour later Chips and the others greeted Woodstock and Stanley by the riverbank. Much to his annoyance, Buzz had been denied an interview with the six on their release and begrudgingly settled for the official statement issued by the department. Needless to say the following headline milked his 'exclusive story' and the ignominious climb down by the department.

On the surface, this looked exactly like the outcome Book had been hoping for; it was over with quickly. But something still needed to be done to get them, and all the others, off the streets.

Unbeknown to Book, one further problem was about to take root at the desk of a researcher in a very high-tech Washington office.

"So you see this flashed up about half an hour ago and at first I thought nothing of it, but then I got to thinking maybe this is some new group we should be watching."

Jeffrey handed a printout of the Daily Rock front page to CIA officer Desmond Grapple, and continued.

"As soon as this paper came out, the group was immediately released because Little Rock's Chief sent an email to the arresting team telling them to charge them or let them go."

Desmond looked puzzled. "So what's so unusual about that?"

"Well it appears that email was never sent or sanctioned by Chief Stuart. Someone got hold of his email signature and spoofed the whole thing. They were out on the streets before anyone knew what had happened, but with the Press still snooping around, and the situation being just a little embarrassing, our local boys decided to let them go and cool things down. Added to which, it was obvious the spoof email was expertly executed from somewhere outside the USA, quite possibly a foreign power, hence our interest. Of course, none of the suspects had access to computers in custody so they couldn't have been charged with involvement or even inciting the spoof email."

This might be just what Desmond had been looking for. His career with the service had been on slow burn for a while now and he needed a chance to raise his profile. The more exotic assignments always passed him by and there had been a string of, what he called, 'bad luck' but his colleagues called bad judgments.

"Good work Jeffrey, see if you can get an ID on any of this bunch and let's get the IT experts onto that spoof email. I'd like a full report on what they can find and their best guesses about who, or where it came from."

"Well, are they out?" Jack demanded, as he charged into the front room on returning from school.

Book replied that they were, due to the adverse publicity in the Daily Rock. "Quite remarkable how quickly the police reacted really."

"Yes!" Jack punched the air and smiled from ear to ear. "I knew it would work."

"You knew what would work?" Honey enquired as she followed her son into the room.

"Well, I said 'leave it to me' remember, and you wanted this over quickly didn't you?"

Honey was beginning to look worried. "What exactly have you done Jack?"

Although Book and Radio had shown little interest in Jack's enthusiastic response and had assumed he was somehow attempting to gain credit for what was clearly down to the press report, they were becoming intrigued now and Honey did look genuinely concerned.

"Well you told me you needed their release ordered from above."

Now he had their attention.

"All I did was a little phishing, some social engineering and a spoof email. That's all really."

Book and Radio were still taking this in as Honey pressed further. "Don't blind me with science Jack, just tell me straight, have you hacked into a system and sent a forged email?"

"Yes"

"Whose email did you forge?"

"The Chief of Police in Little Rock."

"And you said what?"

"I, I mean he, told the arresting officers to charge or release your friends. We knew they couldn't have anything real on them, didn't we?" He turned now to Book, then Radio who blurted in response.

"How on Earth did you do that?"

Jack was about to embark on a full technical explanation of how he learnt his techniques through penetration testing and DDoS mitigation services which 'Black Hole' unwanted traffic, when his mother stopped him with a more basic question.

"Will they find out it was you?"

Jack now looked slightly embarrassed, he had done his best to cover his tracks but the possibility remained that somebody would find the IP address of his Internet service provider and from their records, in time…

"Maybe."

At this point Book's trance was broken and he started to grasp the implications. "But some guy in England just got extradited to the US for illegally entering Government systems. When you say 'maybe' be a little bit more specific will you Jack? By the way, Chips will be proud of you!"

Honey feigned disapproval of this last comment as she'd spent months trying to ensure her son curbed his somewhat clandestine activities in favour of more legitimate endeavours. But then again, she was proud of his accomplishments and she had asked Jack to help.

"It depends." Jack went on. "It depends whether anyone smart enough guessed what I did. It's inevitable the police would find out their Chief didn't order the release and if they struggle with local resources to find out how I did it and where I am, it may take months and they might not ever track me down.

"However, if this gets passed up the line to more serious professionals and they get lucky… Well worst case…"

Jack was interrupted by a knock at the front door.

Silence enveloped the room like a thick fog and the four of them froze. Honey was first to whisper

"Don't say a thing and keep back from the window everyone. I'm going to sneak a look."

She turned and edged on tiptoes towards the hallway and peered out through the stained glass panel on the front door. It looked like a solitary figure, but she couldn't be sure. Nerves already on edge, her heart almost stopped as a crashing sound echoed through the house from the back garden. 'Shit, they're covering the back exit!' Her instinctive reaction, until a cat wailing and then another hissing its reply followed the sound. She edged closer to the door as the blurred image of a hand on the other side thrust out towards her and a second knock hammered at her nerves. The shadow of the figure grew large and the door handle slowly turned.

Honey was at a loss, how could she get Jack out. How could she explain the bizarre circumstances that led to his hacking into an American Police computer system?

The door began to open and the figure was entering her house.

"Wooey, it's only me!"

Raymonde thrust the parcels in front of him as he minced towards her.

"Goodness me dear, you look like you've seen a ghost! Are you all right, you're trembling? I'm so sorry if I surprised you but the things are ready and as I was passing, I thought you'd like me to pop them in. Are the boys here, do they want to try them on? I don't mind waiting."

He did wait and as testimony to his skill, the clothes needed no further alterations. The fact that he was so prompt delighted the household at Primrose Road; well, when they recovered from the shock.

"You two look, how can I put it? You look almost normal." Honey declared undiplomatically when Raymonde left them in their new outfits. Book had discarded his hoody for a red checked shirt and Radio looked quite cool in a bomber jacket and tee shirt, or so he thought.

She continued without waiting for a response. "If we had more time, I'd like to get the scissors on your hair but you'll have to do for now. You'd better get ready."

"Ready for what?" Book queried.

"To leave of course! You don't think we're going to hang around here after that wake up call do you?

Sorry guys but I'm not risking Jack being discovered. We're off, and you'll have to pick up the tab."

Jack looked positively excited at the prospect of bunking off school and going on the run with Book and Radio, but the two of them were still contemplating Honey's words.

"Ok Honey." Book seemed to be coming around. "Ok, I see your point and Jack did stick his neck out for us, but where will we go?"

"Where would you expect hi-tech criminals to take refuge Book? We'll need to get some cash first (predictable) then head for the place I know best, at least for a while."

"How did you know about this place Mum?" Jack enquired as they tucked into the breakfast that Room Service had just delivered.

"Oh just business conferences Jack, you know the sort of thing. Let's eat up and get the others shall we? I need them to go to the bank; I'll feel happier when we've got cash to get us around. We might need to lie low for a while and this place will only do for a couple of days."

Half an hour later, Honey and Jack greeted their fellow fugitives at the junction with the High Street in St John's Wood. Their short journey from Hampstead the previous evening had, unbeknown to them, only narrowly evaded the attention of a British Intelligence Officer assigned to check out 39 Primrose Road by the CIA.

"I've been thinking." Honey grabbed Book by the elbow and led him towards the nearest Bank. "We can't just aimlessly wander around, we need a plan."

They were now in the bank lobby waiting in line for a bank clerk. Next to the queue a young man, appearing to be not much more than a teenager, sat at a desk facing a middle aged woman. Much to her embarrassment, their conversation occupied the attention of most of the queue.

"Mrs Hollister, good to meet you. I'm the new branch manager Micky Davies." This was confirmed by a plastic lapel badge. "I understand you want to increase your overdraft?"

She squirmed uncomfortably as all heads turned with interest. "Yes, that's right but, isn't there somewhere more private?" She tried to whisper.

The line moved up as two of the customers were served.

"Oh don't worry." Micky smiled reassuringly at her. "These days we don't want to be seen as stuffy. It's all open plan, no more quaking in your boots outside the managers office!" He laughed, rather pleased with himself and his role in this new dynamic world. "Now, if you can tell me about your household income, how much you'd like and what you want it for, we'll see what we can do?"

Heads seemed to be inclining with more intent now as the true extent of her discomfort was about to be revealed.

"It's." She leaned forward in desperate attempt at privacy. "It's for my operation."

Neither phased nor abashed, Micky stared at her intently, and urged her to continue. "Go on."

She looked around at the faces in the queue, all seeming to support Micky's interest.

It was then Honey saw an opportunity to jump the queue, the person in front had started to write up a paying in slip but was so absorbed in Mrs Hollister's plight, he was left, hand still hovering and pen poised over the slip, when Honey rushed to the little glass window still dragging Book by his elbow.

"Good morning madam how can I help you this morning?"

Behind them, Mrs Hollister grabbed her handbag and clutching it tightly to her bosom with her head down to avoid any further eye contact, made a dash for the door.

Gasping for air outside the bank, she was still recovering from her ordeal several minutes later when Honey and her entourage walked out, each brandishing a serious number of high denomination notes. Honey took pity and approached her. "How much were you going ask him for sweetheart, maybe we can help?"

Mrs H didn't know whether to run or scream but instead yielded to what she assumed was idle curiosity. "Five thousand if you must know, but I'm never going back in there again."

Radio read the expression on Honey's face and with little prompting, Mrs H was five thousand pounds better off.

Arriving back at the hotel they were feeling quite pleased with their generosity and Honey was much more relaxed about their newfound liquidity. So much so, they failed to notice the smartly dressed intelligence officer seated in a car across the road and carefully observing as they meandered through reception. In fact, he would have gone completely un-noticed had it not been for the overt signal given by the receptionist through the window and caught by Jack, along with the officer's acknowledgement. The others had already reached the lift but Jack had been kneeling below the counter, attending to a wayward shoelace.

When the lift doors opened on the third floor, four white faces peered out.

"You're quite sure, Jack?" Honey implored.

A Remote Farmhouse in Cornwall England, 1st December 2011

"That's the last of them for now!" Book leaned back, exhausted but satisfied with his work.

"Not a moment too soon." Chips replied. "In under two weeks, they'll announce their progress to the world and the last thing we need is a witch hunt."

He was referring to the scientific community at CERN where efforts had continued to produce the first (or so they thought) God Particle; the Higgs boson particle to give it its formal name. The public would be given a verdict on whether or not such a particle will be found in an announcement on December 13th, 2011. Justifying the very substantial amounts of money being spent on the project, by taxpayers of countries on the brink of economic recession, was seen as prudent despite the fact there was nothing to report because, so far, it had eluded them. So a date was set to announce, not the success, but the likelihood that success would follow. A kind of pre-announcement.

The world would have to wait several more months, at least, before actual success would be announced in 2012. Or so they hoped.

In the meantime, almost all the real God Particles had been 'recalled' to Cornwall temporarily from around the World and now at least looked less nerdy. The RAG (Random Appearance Generator) had, at first, produced some interesting results. Random was the operative word and although many of the first guinea pigs lacked any awareness of style, even they drew the line at custard yellow trousers with a bright pink shirt or polka dotted jackets. Honey had been of great assistance in fine-tuning the RAG until the God Particles, or GPs as they now decided to call themselves (largely because of the implied respectability it conferred), could pass for normal human beings. Just two GPs hadn't been through the RAG; Book, because he didn't feel the slightest inclination to change his appearance, and Woodstock, who was yet to show up.

Book and Chips had brought hundreds of GPs through the process and succeeded in modifying the software so that future 'births' would not only produce less nerdy individuals, but it would also be fully automated, allowing Book to concentrate on other things.

The Other thing that was taxing him a great deal was the question of why they were there.

Of course, the simple answer was to do with scientists, accelerators and the quest for Higgs boson. But Book was convinced there was more to it than that.

"Don't worry about the announcement Chips, they're still months away from proving we exist, or should I say, the Higgs boson particle exists. And when they do, the last thing they'll expect to find is us lot.

"Anyway, we've come a long way since London and although the Feds have been a pain, they have at least prompted us to get better organised. We just need to …."

Book was interrupted by the front door crashing open and a very excited Jack running in.

"Come quickly, you've got to see this Book!"

Jack turned on his heels and sped back out into the beautifully laid out gardens. He made a beeline for a bench on the far side of lawn where Radio and Honey were seated. Somewhat insensitively Jack began pointing at the newly improved but rather sad face of Radio.

"Look, tears!" Jack called out.

Honey insisted he should calm down and that it was rude to point.

"Jack, this is not how I brought you up. Don't point like that."

She seemed less concerned about Radio's apparent sadness.

Book, followed closely by Chips, took up a position opposite and stared into Radio's misty eyes. Honey tried to explain.

"I didn't mean to upset him, I just explained that even with his new hunky appearance, I couldn't see us getting together, you know like a couple. He wants us to be like, normal."

Radio looked like he wasn't paying attention to her but she was nonetheless reassured to see from his vacant expression that he wasn't completely devastated, until Book declared....

"That's just not possible!" He paused then continued, "do it again!"

"Do what again?" Honey was puzzled now.

"Make him upset."

"Yeah, go on Mum!" Jack chipped in excitedly.

"What the hell are you two talking about?" Her face reddening. "I don't want, and didn't want to hurt him. There's no way I'm going to make it worse."

Deeply embarrassed, Radio looked up. "It's OK, I know what they're on about. And before you ask Book, I've no idea either but I tell you I can feel stuff, more than we're supposed to."

"Great," Honey pouted, "so you're not bothered about us, just the fact you have feelings. What did you expect?"

It took a little while for Book to explain that GPs should only be capable of quite shallow emotions and the only function of their eyes watering was to clean their lenses. For sometime, ever since they first met in London, Radio had displayed physical and emotional responses well outside his design.

"If Radio has developed more than we bargained for," Chips interjected. "he won't be the only one."

Book pondered, deliberated, then spoke.

"It's to do with our mission. All the time I've been wondering what we're doing here and the answer is obvious."

Nobody else thought so.

"It's about life. We're here to understand human life. All about human life."

Jack was screwing up his face intently as if to improve his brain functioning. "But you guys already know loads about life from everything that's on the Web, how could you find out more?"

Honey was less profound in her response. "How the hell did you get to that conclusion from Radio's emotional state?"

"Both good questions," Book replied, " Let's just say Radio is reminding us that however much is written down and thought to be understood, stuff happens that we can't explain.

"I'll give you an example, take evolution.

"Ever since Darwin's publication of 'The Origin of Species', Scientists have believed the reason for the variety of life forms on this planet has been understood. The process of adaptation through natural selection fully explains how humans became the top species just as it explains why lions are the kings of the jungle."

Chips was starting to glaze over. "Not sure where you're going with this. We all know about evolution and the web is full of detailed explanations."

"No it isn't."

They all looked at Book as if he had finally lost it.

"Darwin, Wallace, the evolutionary scientists, they don't explain how it works - they describe how it works. A description isn't an explanation. Also, logic would suggest that if their 'explanation' was valid, all creatures would inevitably and eventually become humans! Why? Because, the intellectual advantage that has so benefitted humans must also confer an advantage to other species."

"But they've got other advantages!" Jack offered.

"Not that come remotely close Jack. If a tiny amount of improved intellect increased the chances of survival and reproduction, millions of years would result in at least a perceptible difference in all the other species on this planet.

"And let's take the big bang."

"Let's not." Said Honey as she rose to walk back to the house.

But Book persisted. "The obvious questions; what was there before it? And what exists beyond the end of the universe?"

They were all following Honey now but it was clear that Book was getting through, and it was also clear he wasn't about to drop it.

Later that night, when the farmhouse was quiet, Book paced his room and considered the events of the past few years.

They had been lucky to escape from the authorities in London but the chances were that both the CIA and MI5 would be on the trail. In the few minutes gained by Jack spotting the MI5 agent in the St John's Wood hotel reception, they had managed to grab their things and escape through the kitchens onto a back road. With Honey's knowledge of the area, they soon found their way back to the Underground and on to the Mainline railway network.

Cornwall hadn't been their first choice of destination but the small house in Swindon they first rented attracted too much attention from their neighbours, many of whom were convinced the GPs were some kind of religious terrorists. This was understandable as when the call had gone out that the RAG was up and running, dozens of hoodies began turning up in the otherwise boring terraced street. The local police constable started to watch the house and as Book knew many more GPs would soon descend, a frantic message went out and another hasty retreat was bid. As it turned out, this was just a few hours before Special Branch turned up, at five in the morning, deploying armed officers around the hedgerows and parked cars before using a battering ram on the front door and swarming through the house like demented bees.

"Looks like the Brits have lost them again, it's just like before." Grapple complained to his boss, Melissa Worthington.

"Or to be more precise, you lost them didn't you Desmond? After all, it was you who, like last time, told the Brits where to find our mysterious friends wasn't it? And like last time, just a bit too late, yes?" Melissa had never been a great fan of his, especially after the theory she overheard Desmond explaining, near the coffee machine, about positive discrimination and quotas of senior female staff in the service. "Maybe it's time you got out there in the field to prevent anymore mistakes?"

Grapple looked crest fallen, the last thing he wanted was to be stuck in England over Christmas. But he knew Mrs Grapple and the juniors would hardly notice his absence and he did need this assignment to come good for the sake of his career.

There had been one stroke of luck though. Background enquiries into the Little Rock arrest records had turned up one address, and Stanley had returned to visit his parents on precisely the day Grapple knocked on their door.

It seemed that Stanley's short absence, intended merely to collect a few things, had coincided with a mass exodus of his Little Rock friends. At first Grapple got nothing from him, other than confirmation that there was some kind of religious organisation. It was only after Stanley attempted to rejoin his friends, who had by now left for England, that he became a little more cooperative. Stanley assumed, correctly, they had forgotten all about him.

Of course, most of what he told Grapple was of no practical value and other than knowing their leader was thousands of miles away in England, and confirming what they already knew about Woodstock, Chips and the rest of the Little Rock chapter, Stanley's contribution was minimal.

Returning to his office, Grapple reviewed the intelligence with Jeffrey.

"So we know it seemed to start with suspicious behaviour in suburban Little Rock, followed by the unusual sightings on the downtown transportation system."

Jeffrey jumped in at this point. "Arrests were made and one of the suspects, Stanley, was released. The next day The Daily Rock announces a hunger strike."

Grappled continued. "And a sophisticated email forgery was sent from London resulting in the release of the remaining suspects.

"Since then, sightings of similar individuals have been reported in London but the house to which we traced that email has been abandoned."

Back to Jeffrey. "We can't be sure whether or not the London sightings involve the same suspects, but we do know they've been joined by a woman and her son. They escaped from a British Special Branch officer in a London hotel, were next sighted in Swindon but also evaded capture and haven't been seen since."

"So they're on the run." Grapple went on. "We're not sure how many there are or what they're up to but it sure as hell looks like something, and as this started in our homeland, we must assume the risk of whatever it is affects us here."

"What do you make of the boy, Stanley?" Jeffrey asked.

"Hmm, yes the boy, could be up to his eyeballs in it and lying through his teeth.." Grapple liked anatomical metaphors. "... Or he might just have stumbled into this thing and knows nothing about their plans. He just gave the impression they were a bunch of religious loonies. But with that kind of technical expertise, no, there's more to it than that.

"Ok Jeffrey, let's get our arses into gear!

"Book two flights to England for tomorrow, we're going to hunt these critters down."

The 'we' didn't escape Jeffrey who now realised his Christmas was looking increasingly at risk. However, research assistants were rarely invited on operational duties and Jeffrey knew the kudos would help his career, even if it meant spending Christmas the other side of the Atlantic with Grapple.

It was six in the evening, UK time, on December third, when they disembarked at Heathrow Airport and made their way through Customs and passport control. Two hours later, after checking into their adjacent rooms, they met in the hotel bar.

"Any updates?" Grapple asked as Jeffrey wobbled into position on the barstool. This was not only his first trip outside the USA, but one of very few occasions when he'd stayed in a hotel during his twenty-six years. The others had usually been accompanied by his parents apart from on one occasion when he travelled to Washington for his interview with the Agency and partly due to nerves, partly due to general unworldliness, he had drunk rather too much and spent most of the night throwing up in the hotel bathroom.

So he intended to be cautious this time, as he sat there dressed how he thought most young English men would be, to fit into the background; Corduroy trousers, a blue pin stripe shirt and plain black tie with a cardigan and brown leather polished shoes. This compilation of images, combined with his cropped hair and thick-rimed spectacles only served to re-enforce his appearance as a Harvard geek.

Grapple, on the other hand, fitted in exactly with the hotel bar businessperson look. The usual anonymous dark suit and obligatory white collar and tie that normal people would discard at the first opportunity, but in which most business people felt at home.

Of course, Jeffrey had checked base from his room, and the news was positive.

"Yes sir, Mr Grapple…"

"Don't call me that here, Jeffrey. Just stick to Desmond."

"Ok, sorry Desmond. Well I asked the Brits to feed any sightings through to my email address and we've got something that looks interesting in the South West of the country."

"That's cool man, I'm out of here anyway. Now if you can just tell me how to get to Cornwall, I'll hit the trail."

It wasn't the first time a local 'Bobby' had cautioned the owner of a florally painted, bumper attached with string, VW camper van, for parking in the narrow town centre streets but it was more usual during the weeks surrounding the festival. That was one reason it stuck in PC Wainwright's memory, the other was the very untypical appearance of this driver. No Afghan coat or dreadlocks, just a plain looking hoody. Still 'each to his own' thought the somewhat unflappable Constable.

When he returned to the station, he noticed the bulletin seeking information about individuals matching the precise description of the camper van driver. An hour later, patrol cars on the M5 Motorway were on the look out for camper vans heading for Cornwall. You might think that would make it easy for the police but, as luck would have it, a major surfing competition was being held that weekend in Newquay, on the Atlantic coast of Cornwall.

There's something about VW Camper vans and surfers.

As Woodstock sped along the slip road towards the motorway junction at Exeter, several, similarly painted, camper vans were already in the slow lane being overtaken by a large articulated lorry followed by two police cars with sirens blaring. Thinking they wanted him to pull over, the lorry driver slowed and indicated to the left, abandoning his overtaking manoeuvre. This clearly frustrated the officers who abruptly pulled out to overtake him so that they could apprehend their real targets in the camper vans.

As the police cars sped past the lorry in convoy, Woodstock filtered in behind the last camper, feeling at one with the world and his new travelling companions. But when the police cars (now in front of the lorry) signalled frantically at the leading camper, all the traffic began to slow down and, not knowing what was going on, Woodstock overtook the lorry which was now regaining speed. It was clear to the driver that the police were more interested in the campers and as he mumbled something about 'bloody hippies' and the police focused their attention upon their haul of suspect vehicles, Woodstock serenely glided past the commotion, Exeter Service Station, and en route towards the A38 and Cornwall.

Meanwhile, as the police rushed from one vehicle to another desperately searching for someone meeting Woodstock's description, another camper van passed. The occupants waved jovially at their fellow surfers and within minutes a further two more campers passed. Feeling somewhat overwhelmed by the number of suspect vehicles, one of the police officers radioed for assistance. This started a whole new chain of events as a traffic helicopter was immediately dispatched and, as it rapidly approached the final junction of the motorway where the road forked into the A38 and the A30, the wagon train of camper vans was in full view.

Unsurprisingly, they were heading right, towards North Cornwall on the A30 and onward to the UK surf capital of Newquay.

Before long the traffic helicopter was joined by another from a local radio station that had been covering the arrival of contestants for the annual surfing competition, whilst below, on the A30, several additional police vehicles were assisting in the hunt for that elusive driver of one of the many camper vans. The entire entourage was progressing further and further along the A30 as it cut through the wild landscape of Bodmin Moor.

Woodstock, still blissfully unaware of his notoriety, bumbled along the A38 in the same direction, on the other side of the moor. The two roads were set to converge on the moorland town of Bodmin. An aerial view might have shown a collision course if anyone in the helicopter had been checking both roads.

74

Fortunately for Woodstock, they weren't and with the last vehicle cleared a few miles from Bodmin; the police were still shrugging their shoulders when Grapple and Jeffrey arrived on the scene.

"So, absolutely no sightings since he left Glasonbury?" Grapple didn't attempt to conceal the tone of accusation in his question. The police were unimpressed and the most senior officer made that plain.

"We deployed several mobile units, including cars, helicopters and a couple of dozen officers, in order to assist you, without any real understanding of the nature of this emergency or why you consider this individual a threat to anyone. That aside, the only useful information provided was a description of the driver and vehicle. A vehicle, it turns out, painted in much the same way as the dozens of others heading to Newquay for the surf competition.

"However, we'll leave a car in the area in case he appears and check out the camera footage on the Tamar Bridge, in case he took the other main route into Cornwall."

This latter suggestion came up trumps and a couple of hours later, as the darkness of a December evening set in, Grapple, Jeffrey and a small group of officers huddled over a video screen in Bodmin police station.

"As this is a toll bridge, vehicles slow down before crossing. If he'd been leaving, he would've needed to pay, so we'd have got an even clearer picture. But this one isn't bad. Look here he comes now,"

As they peered even closer, the camper van came into sight. Although the camera was mounted high above the road, there was no mistaking Woodstock behind the wheel. His hood was up and he appeared to be singing. They paused the footage to capture this image.

"That's our man!" Grapple announced, as the officers exchanged incredulous glances.

"He doesn't exactly look like a terrorist threat." PC Harris muttered.

Grapple ensured a photo of his prey was circulated to every station in the region and took the bold; some would say stupid, decision to release it to the press.

The next morning Woodstock was all over the local papers accompanied by 'Have you seen this man?' or 'Dangerous terrorist on the loose in Cornwall'.

When he ambled into the Farmhouse, now the last GP other than Book with the distinctive original appearance, the group around the table looked up from 'The Cornishman' daily newspaper on the table in front of them, with decidedly vexed expressions.

This gathering was intended for the popular, rather than scientific Press. Most of the audience had little or no idea about the complexity of particle accelerators or the search for an elusive component supposedly instrumental in the creation of the universe.

All eyes were on the spokesperson, a demure looking lady in her early forties with hair in a bun and, somewhat predictably, wearing a white lab coat. Meanwhile, in conference room one, a bearded man in a sports jacket, delivered the more technical announcement to the scientific community and the more serious press organisations. Yvette coughed to signal that she was ready to begin.

"As you know, we called this meeting to announce the likelihood of success in our endeavours to prove the existence of the Higgs boson particle. This search, if the outcome predicted half a century ago proves fruitful, will confirm that our understanding of the universe is correct. If we're wrong about Higgs boson, then we're wrong about the universe. This particle, thought to be present in the immediate aftermath of the Big Bang, gives mass to all other particles by creating a field that restricts their movement. The larger the particle, the greater the impact the Higgs field will have and therefore the greater its mass.

"Our team has worked meticulously and around the clock since the opening of the new Large Hadron Collider and we're pleased to announce that the progress we've made leaves us confident of a satisfactory outcome in the months ahead. We anticipate this outcome during the course of next year, 2012, but of course, we can't be certain if or when we will discover this elusive particle. In addition to our work here, another team has been conducting similar experiments and both teams have glimpsed something at the predicted mass range in the Higgs field where we anticipate finding Higgs boson. It is tantalisingly close.

"Are there any questions?"

As expected, the very first question from the floor used the term that was guaranteed to make the scientific community cringe - The God Particle.

'What evidence was there of The God Particle's existence; how long precisely will it be before they find it; how can they be sure the universe won't implode?'

The questions came thick and fast, and the answers parried them without a single commitment about anything, just complete confidence it would be found sometime in the year ahead.

When Book saw the news and scrutinised the various Internet reports on this, and the more scientific briefings, he made, what turned out to be, three crucial decisions.

Most of the GPs had wandered off as soon as they had been refashioned but the most recent batch of around thirty of them were still hanging around, coming to terms with their new identities.

That evening, with the new Woodstock resplendent in 'Loons' and an Afghan coat, the remaining group of GPs assembled in one of the barns at the remote farmhouse. Book addressed them all.

"Let's take stock.

"Since the early days when our existence was confined to defragmented anti-matter roaming the information superhighways of the net, we've discovered how to materialise and even managed to automate the process.

"Everyone, except me, has been individualised in appearance thanks to the RAG and we've learned a great deal about this planet, as well as the life on it."

He paused to look around and was satisfied the GPs and his two human friends were paying attention. Some were seated on bales of straw, others stood around the perimeter of the barn, Honey and Jack had made themselves comfortable sharing the seat of an old red tractor.

"However, all is not well,"

There was now a distinct shuffle of uneasiness.

"And I'm not referring to the presence of US agents and the British police closing in on us.

"We have bigger concerns. Firstly, there are too many of us joining an already over-populated planet. The numbers on the inside of the web are growing and it's simply not sustainable to continue. Our automation has been too successful. Secondly.."

He looked across at Radio leaning against the tractor wheel.

"..It's pretty clear some of you have developed behaviours that could only be explained by human emotions, socialisation or biology."

Radio smiled as if to acknowledge Book's logical description and to provide further evidence that he was right. To his surprise, Book was conscious of a facial twitch that could well have been a spontaneous response.

"But the biggest concern is that we have no real idea of what we're doing here, no purpose, no mission. At least, that's what I thought before today."

Outside the barn, noises from the night began to intrude, an owl hooted and the breeze from Bodmin moor stirred in the farmyard. Book looked around again, they were still mostly attentive, although Woodstock was beginning to look uncomfortable, perched precariously on a heap of animal feed bags.

"Sometime in the year ahead, it's likely the humans will work out the real significance of their so called God Particles and, having studied the huge amount of data on the web, I think I know what that might be."

There was an almighty crash as Woodstock slipped off the feedbags and landed ten feet below on the barn floor.

"Sorry man, er just ignore me, everything is cool."

Book did ignore him that is.

"What the humans call God was us lot, well most of us lot, sorry Honey and Jack. Their Higgs bosons sometimes behaving as particles and sometimes as a field, in other words sometimes matter and other times anti-matter, it - that is we were all amalgamated before the big bang. We were God."

At this point the expressions of Book's audience ranged from incredulity to enlightenment. He left a moment for the penny to drop, when it did, a bright young human was the first to voice it. Jack threw his hands up and yelled, "so the big bang was God blowing up!"

"Precisely, and we know the force from that explosion continues to expand the universe. We also know the outward thrust from any explosion eventually diminishes and as it does so, the effects of gravitation forces will alter. In other words, Earth will not remain in a stable orbit around the Sun."

A question from Jack pierced the silent contemplation of Book's audience.

"So how long have we got?"

Honey tried to reassure her son that the timescales were colossal and there was really nothing to worry about, but Chips thwarted her attempts.

"I don't think Book can tell us that, right?"

"That's right Chips. The humans are led to believe the timescales will be, as Honey puts it, colossal. That prevents them from panicking. But the reality is that it could happen today, or in a million years, the Maths are too complex to know, especially when they barely understand the forces in the universe.

"Which brings me back to the Big Bang and Dad."

Now everyone looked confused and several spurted out in unison, "Dad?"

"Yes, well not exactly, er my little joke. Dad, or God if you prefer, blew up creating this universe with all the matter and forces in it but was destroyed in the process."

Chips again. "Should we be reading anything into your choice of words when you say 'this' universe?"

"Very perceptive, Chips. Yes, you should because the universe we, and the humans see isn't the only one. And I'm sorry if that offends your use of language but in this case 'uni' doesn't mean one.

"You see when Dad, alright God, blew it, there was no benchmark of dimensions. No beginning, no end, no start or finish, nobody to experience time passing and no measure of big or small.

"Humans impose these dimensions."

He looked around the barn at the puzzled faces until his eyes fell upon Radio.

"Imagine a radio, not like our Radio over here but the little radio receivers tuned for the masses to listen to. They accept a range of frequencies right? You twiddle a dial and hear all the broadcast stations as the cursor moves from left to right, right?

"Now imagine that human brains are like that, they can pick up and make sense of everything within the range of their dials, or in this case their brains.

"In the case of the radio, there are plenty of other frequencies outside the range of the dial, and if you buy a special Short Wave radio you can hear some of these. In the case of our brains, we can't make sense of anything outside of the range we perceive, so it's hard for us to imagine infinity or a universe with no limits. We don't have anything with which to compare it.

"Back to the Bang, it happened across the spectrum of size not just in the range we are able to perceive. Inside atoms, for example, other universes exist. And our universe may just be an atom in another."

Woodstock was paying attention now. "So you mean our entire universe might just be part of some giant table?" and the idea caught on around the barn "or a compost heap in some giant garden.."

"And there might be another Earth inside my finger nail…"

"Or our universe might be in the flea on the back of a dog…"

"Or…"

Book continued. "Not only that, but you know there are some insects with a lifespan of seconds and mammals like us that live for decades. Our perception of time is also relative, if you'll forgive the pun!" No one got the pun, but once again the idea caught on. Jack was first this time.

"So our universe might be on a plate of food in another, where some giant is about to eat us!

"For him it's a few minutes to eat his meal, for us it's like eternity!"

"Now you guys are on fire, that's exactly what it's like!" Book beamed.

Just as they thought their heads were full, he continued.

"And there's more. You see the frequency doesn't just go in one direction. Matter doesn't just get bigger or smaller, it vibrates at different frequencies. So that much of the time, we can't experience it at all. In fact, we only experience its existence when it falls into our range. At other ranges it's somewhere else and that's what we call anti-matter."

At this point, a number of heads in the barn glanced at each other. Chips, Wiki, Password, Windows, Browser and Blog exchanged furtive glances.

"Oh dear." Chips seemed to be speaking to himself but everyone heard.

"What?" Enquired Book.

"We might have told Stanley about this."

"Stanley?"

"The human who joined us briefly in our cell in Little Rock. We may have implied that we're part of a religious sect that believes in a 'flip side' where matter goes when it's not matter." He, and the rest of his cellmates looked decidedly guilty.

"O…K…." Book sounded a bit like a certain reporter now, by the name of Buzz.

"OK, when the results are finally announced at the LHC and they analyse what they've found, and if the Feds put two and two together, we might just have a problem. But we can't do anything about it now."

*

A few miles away, Grapple and the local police were interviewing a local shop owner. Grapple was holding up the photograph of Woodstock.

"So, you say you've seen dozens of folks matching this description come into the shop to ask for directions?"

"Oh yes dozens over the last few weeks, all looking the same and the worst of it is, they never buy anything. All they want to know is how to get to Mount View Farm. Those Satnav things go a bit wonky around here, and Mount View's a bit off the beaten track, if you know what I mean."

Grapple wrongly assumed he did know what he meant, abruptly left the shop with two local policemen and headed for the two patrol cars. Fortunately, The locals knew exactly where to find the farm and with reinforcements on the way, they set off for Bodmin Moor.

*

Book was coming to the end of his announcement.

"So, you might be wondering what all this has to do with our mission."

"At last!" Honey whispered into Jack's ear.

"It's obvious really. We need to save the universe by reconstructing God, but first we have to kill Radio."

In the moments it might have taken for this information to sink in and a roar of indignation to burst forth from Radio, Jack and Honey, the meeting was interrupted by Wiki gesticulating wildly and making a sound like gas escaping from a burst pipe.

"Shushhh..!"

"What is it Wiki?" Book asked.

Wiki had been leaning against the badly fitting barn door and had noticed lights darting about outside, close to the track which led to the farm from the nearest lane. Unusual because of the remote location.

"Somebody's out there, I saw lights but I think they've gone now."

Book sprung into action.

"I've been expecting this ever since that news report, this is what we do…."

Midnight, Rough Tor, Bodmin Moor, Cornwall

Silhouetted by the moonlight, Book stood on the highest rock on the ancient Rough Tor from where he could see most of the county. A few metres away, Honey was clinging onto Jack as he scrambled to join him.

Their hasty retreat had been made possible by a judiciously parked Land Rover some distance from the farm in the opposite direction to the track that led down from the lane. Book had anticipated the need to leave at short notice and by the time Grapple and his entourage had burst into the barn, all they found was a bunch of normal looking individuals discussing their walking holiday. It helped that Woodstock's camper van had been removed to a disused mine building nearby. With no sign of anyone resembling Woodstock, or the mysterious woman and her son, a dejected Grapple once again left empty handed.

Book's Land Rover was parked off road in nearby woods and at that time on a December night, he knew the only living creatures in the area would be wild ponies or sheep.

Jack finally joined him on the very top of the Tor and stared out over the starlit but deserted moorland; it was an awesome sight. Book was about to explain that these very rocks and the moors around them had survived the Ice Age but Jack had other things on his mind.

"You can't seriously be saying you're going to kill Radio?" A few feet away, Honey expressed her concerns. "Surely not, Book, he's like your best friend isn't he? And anyway what would be the point?"

Book tried to explain.

"Remember, you are both humans but Radio and I aren't and neither are the others. We may resemble you but scratch the surface and we're more like robots than people."

"That's utter tosh!" Honey wasn't buying it. "you know full well that all the GPs have developed their own personalities, especially Radio. He's even shown human emotions."

"And that's why I decided on him. You see Radio is the closest GP we have to being human and.."

"You can't kill him Book!" Jack cut in.

"…And that's why I want to re-engineer him to come back as a human."

This news took a moment to digest. Book stared up at the stars and continued.

"Look up at the sky Jack and tell me what you can see."

"That's easy, stars, millions of stars."

"It's true that you can see some, but many of those bright twinkles in the sky are just the light from stars that ceased to exist millions of years ago. Some were vaster than our own Sun but they collapsed under immense forces into Black Holes and despite the speed of light, it has still taken millions of years for the light to reach us. You see, no matter how large and secure our own Solar System may seem, it can and will cease to exist unless we do something about it."

Honey was confused by most of what Book seemed to be suggesting. "So I've got two questions Book; how do you intend to stop the destruction of our universe, and what's this got to do with Radio coming back as a human?" Although she did secretly warm to the idea of him returning with a full complement of human appendages. Jack too, was feeling slightly more optimistic about the fate of his new friend.

"It's what I said in the barn, we need to re-construct whatever it was that blew up in the Big Bang, what you lot refer to as God. Our GPs, including me, are based upon a single Higgs boson each. It's like our brain is a tiny spec of dust in a control tower that dictates our actions and the movements of our bodies.

When we bring Radio back, every cell will contain a Higgs boson and through that we might just create true consciousness, a soul. That is a dimension the rest of us GPs lack and humans only seem able to access at a very high level.

"Without the full range of human biology, including a real brain and the necessary support systems, we might fail to construct his consciousness. It's a bonus that Radio should also be happier as he already misses much of the human experience, even though he's never had it!"

"So will he still be the Radio we know and…" Honey asked, stopping short of revealing her affection for him.

"Oh he'll be that all right, and much, much more. Radio will be able to access parts of his brain that you other humans aren't even aware of."

"So how will he actually save the Universe?" Jack interrupted.

"We're going to leave that for another day Jack. What happens now is that we'll go back to the farm in the morning if the coast is clear and get ready for one of your Christmas celebrations. Unfortunately only two of you will be able to eat and drink, but the rest of us will make it as festive as possible.

"We'll explain to Radio what is going to happen to him.

"It will take a few months to construct and test the equipment we need to 'reboot' Radio and we must hope that progress at CERN, or the CIA, doesn't force events to overtake us."

All was quiet when they returned to the farm and the Christmas of 2011 was by far the best Jack had experienced. The same could not be said for Desmond Grapple and his young research assistant Jeffrey. They spent Christmas day in a motel close to the A30 and joined a bunch of old age pensioners for lunch.

Grapple had been dreading having to explain their lack of progress to Melissa who seemed to enjoy making snide remarks that this might be a fitting end to his spectacularly undistinguished career. As he made stilted conversation with Jeffrey, during the pensioners' sing song, the only thing that matched his frustration was his determination to find these weirdoes and prove beyond doubt the threat they posed to American citizens.

In the early months of 2012, Book spent most of his time in the barn constructing a sophisticated computer network inside a high tech 'Faraday Cage', designed to prevent any wayward particles from leaving or entering Radio's re-birth.

Meanwhile at CERN, a number of experiments were conducted alongside the search for Higgs boson. It seemed that Book had been right in assuming they would quickly move on to the more meaningful work that arose from the impact of the Higgs field. The search itself moved closer and closer until the news came that a major announcement was imminent.

Coming soon ....

Book 2

Don't miss the next installment, unless you want to.

But if you don't want to, and you are wondering just how Book might save the Universe, or what will happen when they find Higgs boson, or you just want to know about the meaning of life, go to www.booksplace.org and subscribe, you will get notified when the free copy is released for just five days on Kindle. After that, you'll have to pay or live in ignorance.

Acclaimed Books

www.acclaimedbooks.com

Also available from Acclaimed Books Limited

Rachel's Shoe by Peter Lihou
The Causeway by Peter Lihou
Guernsey by Peter Lihou
Passage to Redemption by The Crew
A Covert War by Michael Parker
North Slope by Michael Parker
Roselli's Gold by Michael Parker
Stretch by Brian Black
Last Mission by Everett Coles
1/1 Jihad Britain by Everett Coles
Merlin's Kin by Everett Coles
The Faces of Immortality by Everett Coles
The Last Free Men by Everett Coles
Venturer by Everett Coles
To Rule the Universe by Everett Coles
The Tourist by Jack Everett & David Coles
Druid's Bane by Phillip Henderson
Maig's Hand by Phillip Henderson
The Arkaelyon Trilogy by Phillip Henderson

Coming soon…

Book 2 by Peter Lihou
Larnius' Revenge by Phillip Henderson

Available internationally in paperback and Kindle formats from Amazon and all good book stores.

See the entire catalogue, reviews, author interviews and much more at www.acclaimedbooks.com